PUFFIN BOOKS

THE LAST COWBOYS

Roo lives with Harry Horse and Mandy an old school-house in the Highlands of Scotland. She has turned down several film offers since the publication of *The Last Polar Bears*, preferring instead to concentrate on rabbits. It is her ambition to own one eventually. She is currently working on her first book, provisionally entitled *The Bad Rabbits*.

Harry Horse writes and illustrates children's books. His titles include *The Ogopogo – My Journey with the Loch Ness Monster*, which won the Scottish Arts Council Writer's Award. He is well known as a political cartoonist and has produced cartoons for the *New Yorker*, the *Guardian* and *Scotland on Sunday*. Unusually, rabbits do not play a large part in his life.

D1351141

Other books by Harry Horse

THE LAST POLAR BEARS
THE LAST GOLD DIGGERS

HARRY HORSE

The Last Cowboys

In which Roo searches for her lost

grandfather, a Dog of Some Renown

PUFFIN BOOKS

PUFFIN BOOKS

Published by the Penguin Group
Penguin Books Ltd, 80 Strand, London WC2R 0RL, England
Penguin Putnam Inc., 375 Hudson Street, New York, New York 10014, USA
Penguin Books Australia Ltd, 250 Camberwell Road, Camberwell, Victoria 3124, Australia
Penguin Books Canada Ltd, 10 Alcorn Avenue, Toronto, Ontario, Canada M4V 3B2
Penguin Books India (P) Ltd, 11 Community Centre, Panchsheel Park, New Delhi – 110 017, India
Penguin Books (NZ) Ltd, Cnr Rosedale and Airborne Roads, Albany, Auckland, New Zealand
Penguin Books (South Africa) (Pty) Ltd, 24 Sturdee Avenue, Rosebank 2196, South Africa

Penguin Books Ltd, Registered Offices: 80 Strand, London WC2R 0RL England

www.penguin.com

First published 1999
This edition has been produced exclusively for Nestlé Cheerios and
Honey Nut Cheerios 2003
3

Copyright © Harry Horse, 1999
All rights reserved

The moral right of the author/and illustrator has been asserted

Typeset in 13/15 American Typewriter Condensed

Printed in England by Mackays of Chatham Ltd, Chatham, Kent

British Library Cataloguing in Publication Data
A CIP catalogue record for this book is available from the British Library

ISBN 0–141–31668–3

For Mandy and Roo

My dear Child,

I am writing this letter to you from the airport.
Roo is beside me on her lead and cannot wait to
get on to the plane. I hope that she is well
behaved this time. As you know, Roo is not good
on planes.

We are going to America in search of Roo's
grandfather, an incredible dog by all accounts.

He sailed there on a ship when he was no more
than a pup and after that he travelled all over
America. He has had many different jobs, it seems,
but the last Roo heard of him he was a cowboy's
dog and lived somewhere in the Wild West.

Of course, I have only Roo's word for it, and in
truth I do find some of the stories about her
grandfather a little hard to believe. According to
Roo, he was a famous film actor. She has pointed

1

him out to me on several occasions when we are watching television and, if the truth be known, he looks like a different dog in each one. Roo says that's why he is an actor.

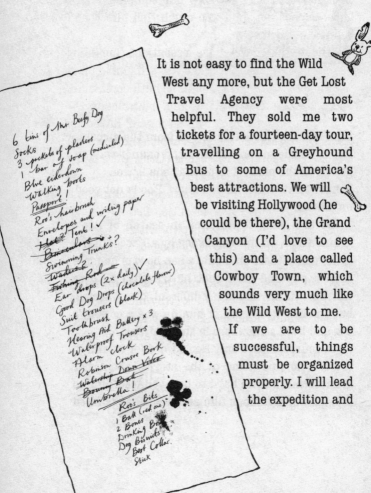

6 tins of Mr Beefy Dog
Socks
3 packets of plasters
1 bar of soap (medicated)
Blue eiderdown
Walking boots
Passport !
Roo's hairbrush
Envelopes and writing paper
~~Hat~~ Tent ! ✓
~~Binoculars~~ ?
Swimming Trunks ?
~~Water~~ ✓
~~Fishing Rod~~ (2 x daily) ✓
Ear drops (2 x daily) ✓
Good Dog Drops (chocolate flavour)
Suit trousers (black)
Toothbrush
Hearing Aid Battery x 3
Waterproof Trousers
Alarm clock
Robinson Crusoe Book
~~Walking~~ ~~Down Vote~~
~~Bowing Boat~~
Umbrella !

Roo's Bits
1 Ball (red one)
2 Bones
Drinking Bo~~~~
Dog Biscuits
Best Collar.
Stick

It is not easy to find the Wild West any more, but the Get Lost Travel Agency were most helpful. They sold me two tickets for a fourteen-day tour, travelling on a Greyhound Bus to some of America's best attractions. We will be visiting Hollywood (he could be there), the Grand Canyon (I'd love to see this) and a place called Cowboy Town, which sounds very much like the Wild West to me.

If we are to be successful, things must be organized properly. I will lead the expedition and

Roo will act as my tracker dog and occasional pack hound.

I have borrowed your Uncle Freddie's new electric golf trolley to carry our equipment in. I hope he does not mind too much. Tell him that I will look after it.

I have taken the bare essentials, including some clothes, the tent and a few golf clubs. I had planned to travel light this time, but I don't think Roo understands what travelling light means.

How can a small dog own so much? Ended up taking: her ball, her plastic rabbit (the one with the ear chewed off), two bones (there were three but I managed to throw the smelliest one away when she was not looking), a drinking bowl, dog biscuits, flea collar (red), best collar (brown with studs), six tins of Mr Beefy Dog, a hairbrush, a tin opener and fork, a bowl with 'Roo' painted on the side in fancy writing, a small chewed stick (why must we take this? I'm sure America is full of small chewed sticks!), a blue eiderdown (quilted) and a beanbag (she sleeps on this, sometimes).

We did not take the garden-ornament rabbit (too heavy), the *Watership*

Down video (this is not a holiday), the bouncy ball (too bouncy), Uncle Freddie's left slipper or the Peter Rabbit cake tin.

Now we must dash. They are calling for us to board the plane. Roo is terribly excited and keeps running around in circles barking. I wish she wouldn't do that! It makes the other passengers nervous.

Will find the old dog and bring him back soon. Tell your parents not to worry. I may be seventy-nine but I am still fit and active.

America, here we come!

with Kind regards,
your Grandfather

P.S. Tell your mother that I have taken my eardrops.

P.P.S. Roo says that she has left a bone under the sofa. Can you 'guard' it for her?

The Hotel Inclusive
1004 Airport View
Los Angeles
California
USA

Room Service 24 Hours a Day.
Just Press the Telephone Touch Pad to Order.

4 October

Dear Child,

We are suffering from jet lag. Hardly know whether it is night or day. At the moment Roo appears strangely bright and is sniffing around our hotel room. She says that it smells good here in America.

5

I'm afraid that I am not really talking to her at the moment as we have had a bit of a row.

She was very badly behaved on the plane. Would not sit still in her seat and kept going into the toilet, where she said that she could hear a mouse scratching. She found an old lady's glove and chewed it to pieces. I had to apologize and give the old lady one of mine, though I don't think that it fitted her properly. Roo barked all through the film, *101 Dalmatians*, and, much to the annoyance of everybody else, kept on making a baby cry by licking its feet. Finally, to cap it all, she got herself stuck underneath a seat and had to be freed by the pilot and three air hostesses. After that she was tied to the seat with her lead for the rest of the flight.

When we landed, we were supposed to head straight to the Hotel Inclusive with all the other passengers, but as we were going through Customs Roo attacked a big grey cat in a travel basket. It caused a dreadful racket and in the panic someone set off a fire alarm. An old man fainted and had to be revived, and we were asked to stay behind and help the police with their inquiries.

When we did eventually get to the hotel, the manager said that dogs were not normally allowed

and that I would have to pay extra for a doggie bed to be put into the room. It cost twenty dollars for the hire of the bed and I knew that Roo was not likely to sleep in it!

At midnight she ran all over the furniture and said that she wanted to chase something. Then she fell asleep on top of the TV. At three o'clock in the morning, she woke up and said she needed her dinner. Half-way through eating it, in mid-bite, she fell asleep. I picked her up and carried her to the doggie bed while she was sleeping. She looked so comfortable and peaceful. However, towards dawn she got up and knocked the phone off the hook. Somehow or other she managed to walk on the buttons that call room service. When I woke up, she had ordered eleven full English breakfasts and some swimming trunks. Very annoyed, as the hotel manager said that I would have to pay, even though it was an accident. I wish Roo would leave things alone.

This afternoon, our tour of America begins. We are going to a film studio to see how a film is made. After that we will have tea in the famous Giant Donut, which I am looking forward to, and then we will board the Greyhound Bus and begin our journey across America.

Will write soon,

love Grandfather

Dear Child,

I am writing this at the back of the bus, so please excuse my handwriting. It is a little bumpy here.

I'm afraid that our tour of Hollywood provided us with no clues to the whereabouts of Roo's grandfather. The people at the studio had never heard of any of the films that he had been in. Neither have I for that matter. I think that I would remember a film called *Invasion of the Space Rabbits*.

Roo chose this postcard as a souvenir. Says that it looks like her grandfather. It looks like Lassie to me.

We visited the pavement where all the famous stars leave their hand- prints. Roo accidentally

9

walked on wet cement and left her paw-prints in a space reserved for Tom Cruise. I don't think anybody saw us. I hope Tom does not mind too much. Tried to sneak away but at that moment a large gentleman with a big cigar shouted at me to stand still. He rushed over, flinging his arms wide, and I was worried for a moment that he was going to attack me. Instead he cried out that he needed Roo's 'face'. Roo told him that her face was stuck to her body and would not come off. Her hackles rose considerably and she swore that she would fight anybody who tried to steal her face.

The man explained that he was Tinkerton T. Thunderbird the Third, or T.T. for short, and told us that he was the biggest film producer in Hollywood. Roo, he announced, was going to be a film star. Taking me by the arm, he steered us into a big black limousine. I must say that I was a bit annoyed. He was not the slightest bit interested in who I was and kept referring to me as Roo's trainer. Told us in the car that he was going to make Roo a household name. She has 'the look', apparently. T.T. drove us ten yards down the road and then we got out. It was hardly worth getting in.

A crowd had gathered to watch us arrive and there was quite a crush at the door to the studio. T.T. held Roo above his head and announced in solemn terms that he had discovered the next big star. The crowd cheered. Some people tried to get Roo to sign their autograph books but T.T. shooed them away and whisked us up to the film set.

The film turned out to be a commercial for dog food. All Roo had to do was to eat a bowl of Crunchy Munchies and then turn to the camera and smile. The film director was a nervous sort of chap. He wore riding boots and a cape, which I thought made him look very silly. He spent a long time with Roo, explaining what he wanted her to do. Roo said that it would come naturally as her breed is renowned for eating, having even won cups for it. Then the director shouted 'Action!' and the filming began.

As soon as the cameras began rolling, things went wrong. Roo ate a little of the food and then started choking. Each time she took a mouthful she made an awful face and looked sick. Then, for no reason at all, she attacked the sound boom. Hung on to it and wouldn't let go. Afterwards, while they repaired the boom, she said that she had thought it was a rabbit swooping down on her. The director got very upset and broke his riding crop against his leg. It took ninety-seven takes and afterwards Roo was sick under T.T.'s desk.

T.T. showed us the door and told me that Roo's career in films was finished. We missed the rest of the tour of the film studios and never got to see the Giant Donut.

We had to take a taxi back to the hotel, pack our luggage and then rush to the bus station to catch the Greyhound Bus.

We waited a long time for the bus to turn up. Roo got very bored and said that she wanted to go home. Had to explain that we could not just go home as we are on the other side of the world. Roo said that she would go on a train.
It was useless trying to explain.

It was evening before the Greyhound Bus pulled up at

our stop. Disappointed that it did not resemble the picture of the Greyhound Bus in the travel brochure. This bus did not have the famous greyhound sprinting along its side. This bus had a picture of a greyhound reclining in a seat. This bus was not made of shiny chrome, but was instead a rather dirty grey. Was this really our bus?

The driver checked our tickets and threw our baggage on. He seemed to be in a great hurry and stopped only to take a look at Roo. Said that she was the smallest greyhound he had ever seen. She is not a greyhound, but I was too tired to argue. It was difficult to make out the other passengers in the darkness. Most of them seemed to be curled up under blankets.

As you know, the brochure says that we will visit the Grand Canyon and after that a place called Cowboy Town. That is where we are hoping to find news about Roo's grandfather. Too tired to write any more. We are on the bus and we are well.

Goodnight,

with love, your Grandfather

Dear Child,

There has been a dreadful mistake. The tickets I booked were for the famous Greyhound Bus, not a bus full of greyhounds! What a disaster!

Caused a terrible racket when Roo woke up and found that she was sharing a bus with over thirty greyhounds. As you know, Roo is not usually good with other dogs. In fact, she does not get on well with any animals, unless they are smaller than she is. These greyhounds are quite large, but

14

actually they are very friendly. However, Roo has been aggressive and quite silly. Keeps growling at them from underneath her eiderdown, even when she can't see them.

To try to distract Roo from the greyhounds, I got her to describe what her grandfather looks like. I think it will help me greatly if I have some idea of what type of dog I am searching for. Unfortunately, this proved to be complicated. First Roo said that he had a big nose, which is not much use at all. Then she said that he was hairy, but most dogs are hairy. I asked her to be more specific and she said that he had a big tail. Really, it is useless.

I am afraid that things are not as they should be on this bus. It says in the brochure that we are supposed to have hot and cold luxury meals three times a day.

Dinner was brought to us by the driver a moment ago. It smells like dog food.

It is dog food!

Another thing . . . Who is driving the bus when the driver is bringing us our meals?

Don't feel very well.

your Grandfather

Dear Child,

I am feeling no better today. I have never been on a bus for so long before. I once went on a day trip to Bognor Regis with your Uncle Freddie and Roo. Roo was just a puppy then and got stuck down a seat while trying to retrieve an empty crisp packet. We had to stop the bus and call the fire brigade to release her. We never did get to Bognor. I should have remembered this before I booked the bus tickets. She has never been good on buses.

She barked at the greyhounds all morning. And most of the afternoon too. It really is getting on my nerves. Each time she sees a greyhound, it sets her off.

This brings me to another matter. I am

17

appalled to report that we are sitting right next to the dog toilet. The queue for the toilet is never-ending. This means that Roo is always finding new greyhounds to bark at. I am heartily sick of it!

Where are we?

The driver never tells us anything.

I hope that this bus will stop soon.

Your Grandfather

Dear Child,

We have arrived at a place called the Silver
Whippet Race Track. No mention of it in the travel
brochure.

Apparently the greyhounds are taking
part in a race this afternoon.
They have been practising all
morning by running up and
down the aisle of the bus. Of
course, this has caused Roo

19

much annoyance and consequently my nerves are in shreds.

The Silver Whippet Race Track was packed when we arrived. The driver was very excited and urged me to bet on his favourite greyhound, Old Slowcoach.

I am not a
betting sort of
man, but I felt it
would be rude not to
enter into the spirit of things. I
promised him that I would bet on Old
Slowcoach, but decided to put five dollars on
a dog called Speedy instead. Roo put a dollar on
the rabbit.

We stood right next to the track to watch the race. The driver's dog, Slowcoach, looked quite fast and came out of the trap with a good burst of speed. Had to hold on to Roo very tight as she was squirming about in my arms with excitement.

Old Slowcoach was miles ahead of the rest of the field. In fact, he was just about to win the race when Roo leapt out of my arms and pounced on the electric rabbit as it flew past. She hung on for ages. I could hardly bear to watch as she whizzed round the track.

I cannot describe her expression. Severe shock perhaps. Then the electric rabbit short-circuited and Roo fell off.

Immediately Roo, Slowcoach, Speedy and all the other greyhounds joined in pulling the rabbit to pieces — all, that is, with the exception of a dog in blinkers, who ran past them and accidentally won the race. Then there was a huge fight, which even the trainers got involved in.

Roo emerged from the middle of this fight with one of the rabbit's pink fluffy ears, looking very pleased with herself. We were put back on the bus by the driver and did not see any of the other races.

Driver in a very bad mood tonight and blames me for what happened today. Everyone on the bus is subdued and quiet. No barking at all, thank goodness.

I cannot wait to get off this bus. I am very hungry and had to eat one of Roo's dog biscuits. Horrible!

With love, your Grandfather

Dear Child,

We were supposed to stop at the Grand Canyon and take in the fine and unspoilt views of one of the greatest sights in America. The driver said that we passed by it last night. He did not like to wake us up so he did not stop. Typical!

It also said in the brochure that after the Grand Canyon we were supposed to visit the famous Cowboy Town. I specifically wanted to go there as Roo said that her grandfather had once belonged to a cowboy called One-Eyed Jack. We might have found valuable clues about him in Cowboy Town.

However, we are not going there now because the greyhounds want to go to a theme park called Rabbit World first.

I don't want to go to Rabbit World!

Told the driver that I thought we should vote on it. The greyhounds won hands down – even Roo cast her vote with them.

It's so annoying. We are supposed to be looking for her grandfather, not gawping at bunnies.

The bus pulled up at Rabbit World and we all trooped off.

I was expecting that Rabbit World would be just a couple of rabbit hutches in a field, but it was

24

much bigger than that. Indeed, it stretched out as far as the eye could see. A man in a rabbit suit met us at the gate and took our money. The place was crammed with dogs and we had to queue for a long time to get on the rides.

My favourite was a roller-coaster ride called the Big Hopper. We climbed into a boat shaped like a giant carrot and then shot down a series of white-water rapids. At the bottom we were catapulted across a lake and after that the carrot boat drifted across the lake in large circles. Roo loved it and went on it three times.

After the Big Hopper we went and looked in the Kingdom of the Rabbits, where the Rabbit King lived. A little train took us underground to see his palace. It looked a bit like a Father Christmas grotto, only with rabbits instead of pixies and gnomes. Of course they weren't real rabbits, they were made of wax, but Roo wouldn't believe me and barked at them the whole time. Eventually a man dressed in a bunny suit asked us to leave. I was quite glad to get out into the fresh air. Roo dragged me off to watch a team of rabbits doing acrobatics in the Fabulous Lettuce Gardens. It was just a lot of hopping about really, but Roo liked it.

I must say that by the end of the day I was getting a little tired of Rabbit World. I didn't want to go and see *Rabbits in Space* — rabbits have never been to the moon.

Ended up going to the Rabbit World Gift Shop, where Roo wasted some money on a rabbit keyring. Why she wanted this I have no idea, as she doesn't even have a key to put on it. In the end I tied it to her collar. She wants me to draw you a picture to show you how it looks.

Still, it was a lovely day and in a way I am glad we came. Roo said that it was her favourite place in the whole world and that she wished we lived there all the time.

Got back on the bus. Driver still in a bad mood with me. Asked rather sarcastically whether I had enjoyed my day with the bunnies. I am going to write a stinking letter to the travel agency about this. Ignored him and went to our seats. Annoyed to find that somebody had chewed a hole in the golf bag.

Sick of this bus. I wish we were in a car. Or a boat. Anything except this bus.

Despondently,

Grandfather

Dear Child,

Hooray! We have arrived at Cowboy Town.

Unfortunately, it is not quite what I had expected. Some of the buildings are just propped-up paintings and it is difficult to tell which ones are real. I think this place was made for tourists.

We watched some actors dressed as cowboys shoot at each other with cap guns. One of them fell off a roof and landed on a mattress which someone had thoughtfully placed there, and afterwards he galloped off on a horse to the applause of the crowd. Then the sheriff rode up and shot all the baddies in a big gunfight. I am sure that Roo thought it was a real fight. She barked all the way through the show and even chased after one of the horses. The horse reared up and the poor chap who was riding it fell off into a water trough, which I don't think was supposed to happen. He looked very angry when he climbed out of the trough, but the crowd loved it and some children thought Roo was part of the show and had their photographs taken with her.

I decided that we would ask in the saloon if anybody had seen One-Eyed Jack or his dog. But the saloon turned out to be a coffee shop and the waitress said that nobody by that name had been in this morning. When I explained that One-Eyed Jack was a cowboy, she said that the Lassoing Demonstration started after lunch. I'm looking for a real cowboy, not some actor dressed up as one.

After that we wandered up the main street and looked in some shop windows. You can buy all sorts of things in Cowboy Town. Mostly Stetson hats, Western shirts and cowboy boots. Roo was very taken with a plastic rabbit in a cowboy hat, but I'm afraid that I had to put my foot down. We don't need to drag a rabbit in a cowboy hat around with us. I bought some beef jerky instead, as the chap in the shop said that this is what real cowboys eat. He said it was strips of dried beef, but it tasted like old boot leather to me. It was too tough for my teeth, I'm afraid.

However, Roo said that it was good meat and swallowed her piece whole – you are supposed to chew it slowly!

After lunch (spare-rib bones – delicious!) Roo wanted to see the Bucking-Bronco Contest. We followed all the other tourists to a large paddock with a fence around it.

I have never been to a Bucking-Bronco Contest before. The idea, it seems, is for the rider to stay on a wild horse while it leaps about. They have no reins or saddle to hold on to, just a belt around the horse's middle.

We watched quite a few cowboys get thrown into the air by their broncos, and one poor chap was kicked in the bottom by a yellow horse when he fell off. Told Roo to stay by my side at all times as it looked quite dangerous.

Then a rider called Lonestar Jackson came out on a big red horse and I must say he was very good. He stayed on for a whole minute, which seemed to be a record. The crowd went mad. Looked about to see where Roo was and discovered that she had gone!

Searched anxiously up and down the aisles but she was nowhere to be seen. I became very worried and found myself asking everyone if they had seen a little dog. No one had. There was

31

suddenly a great cheer from behind me. I looked back at the show and saw an incredible sight. A small fat pony was galloping round and round the ring, and hanging on to it was Roo!

The crowd were cheering, and the more noise they made the faster the pony galloped.

Roo was slipping on and off, sometimes scrambling all the way underneath the pony, only to reappear on the other side. At one point she even ended up on the head of the pony.

At last the little pony decided to stop and eat some grass. Roo fell off.

The announcer was beside himself with excitement and told us that the time was a new world record.

Quite a mob of people wanted to shake Roo's paw. I had to wait for nearly two hours while she was carried about on their shoulders. I eventually managed to drag her away, only to find that the bus had gone without us. The driver had dumped Uncle Freddie's golf trolley and our bags outside the saloon.

I blame Roo for all this. If she had stayed by my side during the Bucking-Bronco Contest none of this would have happened. I don't know how she got on to the pony in the first place. Roo explained that a mouse had lured her away to a big mouse hole and there she had walked on what she thought was a brown carpet. The carpet suddenly turned into a pony and galloped off with her.

I didn't want to hear any more.

I am posting this letter to you from the Cowboy Town post office. It is just about to shut.

Don't worry, Child. We will be all right. We are fortunately prepared for an emergency of this sort. We have the tent, the golf trolley and a little food.

We will hitchhike back to Los Angeles instead. I have seen this done in films. It should not be too difficult.

With love,

Your Grandfather

11 October
On the way back to
Los Angeles

Dear Child,

It is very difficult to hitchhike with a dog.

Every car that did slow down was soon driven away at high speed when people saw Roo with me. I do not blame them. She was straining on the lead and acting like a mad dog.

Decided to hide her behind the golf trolley and this seemed to work, for a large camper van stopped and a very pleasant couple called Bob and Miriam invited me to ride with them. They were not keen on having a dog as well, but I persuaded them that Roo was very well behaved normally. Bill agreed if Roo sat in the back of the camper.

What a stroke of luck! They are going to Los Angeles and are even planning to stop at the

Grand Canyon on the way. So I will get to see it after all.

Bill and Miriam are excellent company and we all get along like a house on fire.

It is a shame that Roo has to ride in the back, but dogs make Bill nervous. Roo keeps moaning that she wants to be in the front, but I am sure that she is comfortable back there. It's better than walking.

To be honest, Child, this is the best way for our journey to work out. We have only a few more days left in America. I realize that it was ridiculous to think we could ever find a dog in the vastness of this country. Impossible.

I will tell Roo in the morning that the search is off. We are parked up in a lay-by and my tent is pitched next to Bill and Miriam's camper van. Must go, because Bill wants me to go over the Grand Canyon brochure with him.

Having a lovely time,

your Grandfather

Dear Child,

What a wonderful day!

The Grand Canyon was breathtaking. Locked Roo in the camper van as I didn't trust her near the edge of the canyon. She could have fallen in. Instead I left her with a packet of beef jerky to chew on.

Tonight Bill chose a very pretty spot called Wilderness Gates in which to make our camp. Marvellous views over a lake, surrounded by a huge forest.

Pitched tent in a clearing and made our evening meal. Roo wouldn't eat her own dinner and I was rather annoyed to see her going over and pestering Miriam for spare-rib bones.

I tried to call her back, but she pretended not to hear me. Miriam was very relaxed about the whole thing and as the sun went down we sat around and chatted. Roo crunched on a bone under the table and came out only to tell us about her grandfather.

I sometimes wonder whether I really want to meet the old dog. Roo told us a dreadful story about how he had lived in a cave with an old bear and in the end smelt so bad that he could clear out a whole town just by walking through it. When everyone had fled, he would help himself to all the food they had left behind. As if that was not bad enough, she then started on about how he was an outlaw dog and used to rob stagecoaches by pouncing on them out of trees. Bill looked quite upset and had to go and lie down in the camper van.

Told Roo that Bill and Miriam did not want to hear any more horrible stories about her grandfather. This caused her to go into a sulk and, before I could stop her, she had slunk off into the forest.

As I write this the sun is going down and Bill is putting away the camping table. Roo has still not come back. I have called and called her name, but there is no sign. I hope that she is all right.

Actually a bit – no, *very* – worried,

Your Grandfather

Dear Child,

I am pleased to say that Roo did come back last night. Unfortunately she was not alone.

I was just putting my pyjamas on, when she charged into the camp followed by two very angry skunks. They made a dreadful smell and most of it managed to get on to Roo's coat. She bolted into the tent and tried to get it off by rolling on my clothes!

The smell is appalling. Had to wash Roo in the lake, but the water was cold and she did not like it much. Even after her bath she still smelt awful. I tried to disguise it with some aftershave, but I think perhaps that made things worse.

40

Took Roo back to the camper van and explained to Bill and Miriam about the skunk incident. I do not know what I said to upset them, but they rolled the windows up and drove off very fast, leaving us behind. They didn't even say goodbye. Now we are stuck here without a lift. This is all Roo's fault!

Packed up the tent with a heavy heart. We have no other option than to walk now. I doubt that anybody will want to stop and give us a lift. I cannot hitchhike with a dog that smells like a skunk. Roo said that she preferred walking anyway. I did not bother to say what was on my mind, as I do not want another argument.

We walked all morning along the road. Very few cars passed us and although a pig farmer did stop, he drove off again when he caught a whiff of Roo.

About lunchtime, we came upon the most unusual diner at the side of the road. It was called the Big Egg and was run entirely by chickens.

Caused a lot of fuss when I walked in with Roo, because they thought that she was a fox. Had to explain that she was not and promise I would be responsible for her.

When they had all calmed down, we took a look at the menu. All the dishes were made from eggs. There were fried eggs, boiled eggs, poached eggs, scrambled eggs, even egg burgers and egg milkshakes. We chose fried eggs on toast and were very surprised when a hen came to our table with a frying pan, laid two eggs in it and then fried them. It's a bit shocking really to see your food presented like this. I'm not sure if I enjoyed it. Afterwards Roo asked a hen why roast chicken was not on the menu and that was when they asked us to leave. She can be very thoughtless sometimes.

We pressed on until we came to a crossroads. Had no idea which way we should go. The sign at the crossroads was a little confusing. It had many names on it, but not one mention of Los Angeles. In the end we took the road to a place called Homeward Bound, because it sounded more promising than Swampduck or Pretty Ugly.

The afternoon got hotter and hotter, so we stayed under the shade of a tree for an hour to cool down. It is important in heat like this to drink plenty of water. The sun can be a killer and dry you out in no time at all. Told Roo that the human body is made up of over 90 per cent water. She said that a dog was made of 100 per cent, which is impossible. You would float off if you were made entirely of water.

The going was tough for the rest of the afternoon. The road was very dusty and full of

holes. I had to keep stopping for Roo as she insisted on inspecting every rabbit hole we went past. Told her that we have no time to look down rabbit holes. After that she sulked and pretended we were travelling separately. We walked along the road in silence.

The golf trolley seemed heavier each and every time we went up a hill and Roo never offered to pull it once. She is supposed to be helping me.

Eventually we made camp between two pine

trees and pitched the tent. The moon came up and threw a ghostly light on the road. I write the last of this letter by the light of my last candle in the tent. Roo is asleep in my sleeping bag. How will we get home?

Anxiously,

Your Grandfather

what a mess!

14 October

Dear Child,

I did not sleep well last night. Something was rummaging about outside the tent. I am certain that it was a bear. Bears can be dangerous, you know, so I thought it best to lie low and keep still. Roo slept through the whole thing, which in a way was fortunate.

Got up at dawn and peered out of the tent. The camp was in a dreadful mess. Pots tipped over and my clothes strewn about. All of Roo's dog biscuits have been eaten and two pairs of clean socks have gone. Roo claimed to be upset at the loss of the biscuits and resigned herself to a diet of spare ribs instead. Now we don't have any spare ribs!

Packed up what remained of our possessions

and continued along the road. We did not see a single car all day long and the only signpost I noticed was for a place called Big Mud.

No sight of the bear all day, which is good. However, I have pitched our tent in front of a large boulder, so that we can have some protection from the rear in case the bear decides to come back and attack us.

Very worried, Child. Roo is on guard and appears quite fierce. Her hackles are permanently raised and she is walking around the camp in a strange stiff-legged way. We will fight to the death if needs be. I have my one-iron golf club ready.

Goodnight, Child.

Grandfather

15 October
A Heroic Spot
(Not on Map)

Dear Child,

I tried to stay awake and on guard last night. But I'm afraid that I nodded off into a lovely sleep soon after midnight. Awoken by an almighty crash. A terrible commotion was going on outside the tent. The bear was back!

My first thought was for Roo. But my dog was not with me in the tent. All that remained was her collar and the rabbit keyring. Where was she? Then I heard a bark. She was outside with the bear!

I listened to the dreadful grunts and growls, most of them from Roo, and I feared that she was fighting for her life. Then suddenly all went quiet.

My poor dog . . .

I steeled myself to expect the worst. With a heavy heart, I was just about to open the flap when I felt something scrabbling at the foot of the tent. The bear was trying to get in . . .

My first reaction was to strike with the golf club, but terror gripped me and I remained rooted to the spot. The bear was now squeezing through the tent flap. I prayed that the end would be swift.

I cannot describe my joy when I saw that it was not a bear, but my own dear Roo. She was very muddy and her coat was in a terrible mess. I wrapped her in a blanket and cleaned her up as best I could, while she licked my face and told me all about her fight with the bear. How the bear had crept up on her and then pounced and jumped about on her. How they had fought for hours and hours. How at last she had struggled free and overpowered the bear.

My dog is a hero and deserves an award. Maybe a medal or a certificate for bravery. Roo said that a few spare ribs would do. What a brave dog!

It is dawn as I write this. I have not been out of the tent yet. I do not relish the idea of seeing the dead bear lying out there. Roo is very bruised and cannot sit up. I hope that the bear did not hurt her insides. She has just told me that she did it to save my life.

A sketch of a brave dog!

What a brave dog!

When morning came at last I got ready. Told Roo to remain in bed. She has been brave enough. Prepared myself to take a look at the bear. Armed with the golf club, in case the bear was wounded and ready to attack, I ventured out.

I was terribly shocked by what I saw outside the tent. There was no dead bear stretched out on the ground. Instead, lying on its back in the midst of much wreckage, was a small duck.

At first I thought that this poor creature was another victim of the bear and I must say that I felt angry. I lifted the duck up and it gave a feeble quack. This brought Roo out of the tent. When she saw the duck, she bolted back inside. It has all become very clear to me now.

Took the duck into the tent and gave it a drop of brandy mixed with milk. Roo skulked about under my feet, pretending not to notice that there was a duck in the tent. She seems to have made a full recovery and even wondered what was for breakfast.

We are setting off now, so I shall write no more. The duck is at least awake and seems a little better.

A bear indeed . . .

love Grandfather

Dear Child,

I am writing this letter to you from One Horse Town. We came upon it yesterday at the end of the road. I have no idea what lies beyond as the road stops here.

One Horse is not a big place. There is only one street and a collection of sorry-looking buildings in need of some repair. I found a saloon called Grogman's, a general store and a diner called the Hungry Horse.

Went with haste to try to find a telephone to call the airport.

But One Horse has no telephone and the chap in the general store said that the only form of communication in this town is handled by the Pony Express. I have heard of the Pony Express. Long ago letters and messages were delivered in America by a man on a fast pony. All that remains now are the fast ponies. A bunch of them were hanging around outside the general store and there was a bit of an argument over which one of them was going to carry my letters. A small fat pony won the argument and went off at a slow trot. I hope they get to you.

The chap in the store says that a train does pass through occasionally. Unfortunately we have just missed one — it came through yesterday. However, he is certain that another train will arrive in the next few days and is sure that it will be going to Los Angeles.

We have taken a room over the saloon for five dollars a night, paid in advance. The owner, a shifty fellow who introduced himself as Grogman Junior the Third, 'owner of the finest little saloon west of Cowpoke', charged me two dollars extra for Roo and fifty cents for the duck. Our room has a balcony and looks out on to the main street. The bed is a bit lumpy and the only washing facilities are a cracked porcelain bowl and a chamberpot.

Grogman Junior warned that we were to keep the noise down and that visitors were not allowed after nine. I doubt that we will be having any visitors. We don't know anybody here.

This evening we had a meal in the Hungry Horse. I was a bit surprised by the menu. Hay burgers and hot oat mash are not really my thing. Roo was very disappointed that there were no spare ribs. We ended up eating apple pie, which was all I could find that didn't have pony nuts in it. I mixed up some corn and fed the duck from a spoon. It really appears to be a lot better and has actually become quite attached to Roo. I think I will call it Boo, because it gave Roo such a fright. Roo not at all amused.

The saloon was quiet when we got back from the Hungry Horse. Went to bed at about ten o'clock.

Do not worry about us, Child. Although we will miss our flight, I am sure that when we get the train back to Los Angeles we can sort the whole thing out.

With love, your Grandfather

17 October
One Horse Town

Dear Child,

Woken out of a blissful sleep by the sound of many
hoofs. Staggered to the window to see a big herd of

horses galloping up the main street. Must have been over twenty of them. A couple of them saw my golf trolley hitched outside the saloon and started kicking it to pieces. By the time they had galloped off the golf trolley was in a very sorry state. I am dreading having to explain to Uncle Freddie what has happened. How can I tell him that a gang of horses destroyed his golf trolley? He will never believe me.

These horses are a complete nuisance. They call themselves the Riderless Horses and are a type of gang. Grogman Junior told me that so far they have held up a grain merchant's and stolen a consignment of hay and oats from an agricultural store. The old sheriff got so fed up chasing after them that he moved away and opened a cat-food shop in Catville. Now One Horse has no sheriff and the Riderless Horses run riot all day long.

I think it best if we stay out of their way while we wait for the next train. Went up to our room this afternoon and lay on the bed. I read aloud from *Robinson Crusoe* to Roo and the duck. I think the duck enjoyed the story because it quacked loudly at the end of every sentence, but Roo was far too busy staring out of the window to pay any attention.

Robinson Crusoe is a marvellous book about a man marooned on a desert island. Roo said that it can't be that marvellous because it doesn't have any rabbits in it. Tried to explain that not all books have to have rabbits in them, but according to Roo a book without rabbits is not worth reading. Sometimes she can be very ignorant, you know.

I am finishing this letter in the room and at last the horses are peaceful. There was a big fight earlier outside the Hungry Horse. It went on for over an hour and then they suddenly stopped and went inside for something to eat. Then they came out and started all over again. Roo watched the whole thing from the balcony and at one point jumped off and joined in with them.

It is now ten o'clock and they have at last stopped. Roo has only just come back upstairs to have her dinner. Bolted it down very fast and went back to join her new friends. The duck scrambled after her. Friendship with these unruly horses is something that I want to discourage.

When Roo got back at midnight, I told her off. She paid not the slightest attention, flopped on the bed and went to sleep. The duck made a nest out of the pillow, ignoring the box of straw, so there is little room for me.

Will send this letter in the morning by the Pony Express.

Hopefully a fast pony will deliver it.

Do not worry about us, Child. The train will come soon.

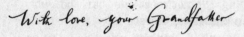

With love, your Grandfather

Dear Child,

Bad news. The Riderless Horses have elected Roo as the new sheriff. I think it ridiculous that a small dog should even be considered for the position. Roo said that her breed was the obvious choice, being renowned as sheriffs. What nonsense! There are police dogs, it is true, but I have never heard of a sheriff dog.

I ordered her not to accept the position and told her that, thankfully, the train is due tomorrow morning and we will be on it.

Very annoyed later to see that she had disobeyed me and was wearing

61

the sheriff's star on her collar. It really is not good enough. We are supposed to be making our way back home, not getting involved in a lawless town overrun by gangs of wild horses.

Roo is not even a very good sheriff and I'm afraid that the position has gone to her head. She spends most of her time swaggering up and down the main street, followed by the duck, who seems to have appointed itself her deputy. How can a town be governed by a dog and a duck?

It is evening as I write this. Roo and the duck are downstairs in the saloon. Roo says she needs to keep an eye on things. If you ask me, she has made the atmosphere even worse since she became sheriff. Heard a terrible commotion at about eleven o'clock and looked out of the window to see Roo, the duck and a gang of horses charging up the main street after a big tom cat, whom they ran out of town.

At midnight a goat was thrown through the saloon window, which fortunately was open at the time, but the glass was shattered when he leapt back in. The fighting stopped around one o'clock and general tuneless singing began.

I will send this letter in the morning, if it is safe to cross the street to the general store. If the train really does come tomorrow, we can at last get out of One Horse and back to Los Angeles.

Grogman Junior has given me

his word that he will look after the duck for us when we leave.

I had to give him a dollar for its lodgings, nevertheless. Roo and the duck are still downstairs in the saloon. I am turning the light off.

With love, your Grandfather

Dear Child,

Good news and bad news, I'm afraid. The good news is that the train turned up. The bad news is that it was a mule train. Twenty mules in a long line, each laden with provisions. I did not even consider asking them for a lift.

Roo is no longer the sheriff of One Horse. She got sacked for letting the Riderless Horses rob the Hungry Horse last night. It is rumoured that a dog and a duck were also seen carrying food out of the diner. Worse,

65

WANTED
MAD-DOG ROO
FOR ROBBERY

she is now considered an outlaw by the new sheriff (Grogman's cousin, T. Grubman Junior) and there is even a wanted poster of her outside the saloon. Hard to recognize it as Roo as someone has drawn a moustache on her!

This is all very worrying, Child.

I have decided that we must leave One Horse tonight. Roo quite upset when I outlined my plans and said she wanted to stay and fight. Said that a dog had to do what a dog had to do, whatever that means. I told her to lie low, preferably under the bed.

WANTED
'THE KID'

I spent the last of my traveller's cheques on provisions from the general store. Bought some tins of beans and sausages, as there was little else to buy. Went back to the hotel and found that Roo was not lying low as I had ordered but playing a game of cards with the Riderless Horses in the saloon bar. The duck was waddling about on the piano keys, making a terrible racket. So much for lying low!

Those horses were dreadful cheats and kept

hiding cards in their saddles.
One horse laid down five aces and
won a big pile of money. Nobody
seemed to notice that there are
only four aces in a pack. Roo is not
a good card player. She seemed
pleased that she had lost twenty dollars
in order to win two.

When everybody had gone to bed we
sneaked out of town. I'm afraid that we had to go
back and take the duck with us when I saw that
Grogman had advertised in his window that
tomorrow's special was 'Duck à l'Orange'.

We left the remains of Uncle Freddie's golf
trolley outside the saloon tethered up to the
hitching post. It is so badly damaged that there
was no point taking it with us.

We followed a dusty track out of town.
Fortunately the moon was full, so we could see
where we were going. I was worried that the new
sheriff might send out a posse to capture Roo.
Roo said she was not frightened of
any possum and would fight it. I
had to explain to her that a posse is
a party of deputies gathered to hunt
outlaws. Roo said she would fight a
hundred possums if she had to. I

don't think she understands how serious the situation is.

It is nearly dawn. We are hiding behind an old water tower and fortunately nobody seems to be after us. The duck keeps quacking for no good reason. It's making me nervous.

your Grandfather

Dear Child,

We are lost, Child, and I have no idea where we are heading. Roo says that her natural instinct will get us home, but it is more likely to lead us down a rabbit hole.

Followed a track all day with Roo leading the way. Had to carry the duck as it could not keep up. It unravelled a hole in my cardigan and stuck its head inside.

A cold wind blew all day.

Made a big fire and cooked the sausages and beans.

I did not even bother to pitch the tent as the ground was far too hard to drive in a tent peg. Made our beds as comfortable as we could. The duck nestled under my arm and Roo snuggled up against my back.

This is a lonely and desolate place.

Maybe we should have stayed in One Horse and faced the consequences. All this is Roo's fault!

Very down tonight, Child.

21 October
Somewhere

Dear Child,

Woken in the middle of the night by Roo and the duck walking on me. Gave me a fright, I can tell you. They were both very panicky. Indeed, I couldn't get a word of sense out of Roo, who kept gibbering something about a big cow.

I heard a faint rumble of thunder.

The thunder grew louder and suddenly our camp was swamped by a tide of animals. There were elks, moose, herds of caribou and white-tailed deer. Swarms of much smaller animals began to appear and throughout the night there was a lot of squeaking as they marched into our camp. I saw coyotes and racoons, chipmunks and porcupines, even prairie dogs and muskrats streaming through. At one point I thought that I glimpsed the Riderless Horses galloping along the ridge. Then a huge eagle soared overhead, followed by flocks of smaller birds, and soon the sky was full of beating wings. The duck was very keen to fly at this point and tried to take off to join its fellows, but

the effort was too much and it landed on some mice instead. Fortunately nobody was injured.

I have never seen so many animals, not even in a zoo.

Suddenly the sky was lit up with a tremendous flash, as if a giant star had exploded, and all the animals fell to the ground and cowered. A giant buffalo made of stars appeared in the night sky. As it galloped across the sky, the animals gasped in unison. It lifted its starry head and gave a great bellow that shook the ground.

As if in answer to his call, all the animals hooted, howled, barked and quacked back to the star buffalo. I even found myself calling to him, and the only thing I could think to shout was 'Hooray!' which in retrospect sounded rather silly. The star buffalo shook his great head, snorted and then slowly turned and began to gallop towards the dawn.

He has gone now, Child, but the animals are still restless. Roo says that we must follow the cow, who is calling us to the wild. I have no idea what she means . . .

Dear Child,

We followed the animals all day. We were joined by a racoon and a beaver who tagged behind for a while. We lost them in the evening, as the first flakes of snow began to gently fall. I twisted my ankle in a rabbit hole as we climbed into a great forest, and after that I found it difficult to keep up.

The last stragglers disappeared into the trees and we found ourselves alone again. When the snow got really bad, we crawled into small dark cave and there I made a miserable fire to try to keep us all warm.

We have eaten a few sausages and we feel a little better. It is very cold in here.

Very tired now, Child. We will rest a little while . . .

Dear Child,

I am writing this to you from inside the cave. It is still snowing and the sound of the wind in the trees is lonely and terrible. Roo and the duck are snuggled beside me in the sleeping bag.

I have no idea where we are and my ankle is so swollen that I can hardly walk another step.

I feel a little scared.

When I look at Roo, for a moment I am filled with courage. We have been through some tough old scrapes together. But this time, I really believe the chips are down, as they say. We are lost in the wilderness of America and nobody knows where we are.

I am going to leave this letter for you inside the cave. If someone finds us after we have gone, then I hope that they will send it to you.

Do not cry for us, Child. Roo heard the call of the wild and it led us here. There must be a purpose behind it.

Now we will sleep. The fire is dying and there is no more wood. I can feel Roo beside me in the darkness. I am with my dog and I am happy.

Goodnight, Child.

We'll see you in our dreams.

My dearest Child,

As we lay in that cave by the dying embers of the fire, Roo whispered that she wanted me to sing her a special song. I took her in my arms, as I have done since she was a puppy, and I sang to her. The song went something like this:

'I have a dog and her name is Roo,
Bet you five dollars she's a good dog too!
Yes, I have a dog and her name is Roo,
She's the best old dog I ever knew!'

I had just finished the first verse and was going to sing the bit about all the rabbits that she had ever chased when I thought I heard music in the wind. At first I wondered if my ears were playing tricks on me, but then I saw that Roo and the duck could hear it too, for they both sat up and listened. There. Singing. Somebody was singing our song, but the words were slightly different. Their song went something like this:

'I have a dog and his name is Blue,
I bet you TEN dollars that he's better than Roo!
Yes, I have a dog and his name is Blue,
He's the best old dog that I ever knew!'

I cannot remember how I got to my feet.

We scrambled out of that cave as fast as we could and looked out across the clearing.

There, seated on a fallen pine tree, was an old man strumming a banjo. At his feet was an old grey dog.

Roo started to bark and the old dog looked over in our direction and began barking too.

I cannot describe what happened next. All I can

say is that I have never seen Roo so happy. She ran round and round in circles and then sprang across a stream towards the old dog.

The two dogs met in the clearing and jumped on each other, rolling and tumbling in the snow, licking each other's faces and wagging their tails so much that I thought they might take off and fly.

We have found Roo's grandfather!

The old man helped me back to his cabin in the woods. There he bandaged my ankle and made us an enormous meal. Lashings of cornbread for the duck; ham, fried eggs and stuff called grits for me (delicious!); and, to Roo's delight, a big pile of spare ribs. Roo's grandfather, or Old Blue, as he likes to be called, ate as much as all of us put together and then he spent a long time grooming Roo until her coat shone. The old man told me the story of how he found Old Blue many years ago, wandering in the forest, alone and starving. He must be terribly old, because he looks very grey.

The old man, whose name is Ted, reckoned that Old Blue was fifteen, which is very old for a

dog. Old Blue interrupted and said
that he was exactly a hundred
years old, but I think that may
have been in dog years. More probably
it was like the rest of his stories, most of which
I still find hard to believe.

Old Blue, with Roo curled at his feet, went on to
tell us some of these stories. He described how he
had been swallowed by a whale at Cape Cod, and
had enjoyed it so much inside the whale that he
had stayed for a year. Another story followed
about how he had been squashed so badly by an
elephant seal in Newfoundland that for six
months he looked like a four-legged pancake. After
that, he told us, he had worked for a mule-skinner
and was kicked so hard by a mule in Alabama that
he had ended up in Georgia. He even told us that
he had worked for the President of the United
States as a secret agent, had been to the moon
with an astronaut called Bud and had sailed down
the Mississippi on a guitar. Lastly, he recounted
his days spent as an outlaw with the famous One-
Eyed Jack, the meanest cowboy who had ever
roamed the West.

Proudly, Old Blue told us that he
and One-Eyed Jack were the last

cowboys left in America.

Then One-Eyed Jack had been thrown in gaol and Old Blue wandered the trail, alone and starving. If Ted had not found him, he would surely have died.

All the time Roo looked up at her grandfather with admiration, wagging her tail vigorously at the best bits. At last Old Blue grew tired and lay down to take a nap. Now I know where Roo gets her snoring from.

It is evening as I write this, Child. Roo is curled up next to her grandfather. Occasionally she sits up and wags her tail, almost as if she cannot believe that we have found him.

Goodnight, Child,

with love, your Grandfather and Roo

Dear Child,

You will be pleased to learn that my ankle is much better. I can walk short distances with a walking stick and a little help from Ted.

He is a marvellous host and this afternoon he showed me around where he lives. His house is a bit ramshackle, but at least it is comfortable and warm. He has no TV or radio, and he told me that he never gets much in the way of company passing through. I think he was very glad to catch up on the news of the outside world. We hardly saw Roo and Old Blue at all. They had a lot of dog stuff to do, it seems, and spent a long time digging in rabbit holes.

Of course, I am still worried about how we will

get back home. Ted has heard of Los Angeles, but his description of how to get there sounds a little vague. He says that he is going to do some serious thinking about it, though.

Tell your mother that we are missing her. But please tell her that we are well. I don't want her to worry. Ted says that we can send this letter in a bottle down the stream and that it's bound to find you somehow. I think I'll wait until we find a proper post office.

Roo and I are coming home soon, I promise.

with love,
your Grandfather

Dear Child,

I do like it here, but I wish that I was back home now. Ted has been so kind, but in truth I doubt that he knows how to get to the nearest town, let alone Los Angeles. The snows began again today. Covered the whole wood in a thick white blanket. It was very beautiful to look at, but it has made it much colder here. Only Old Blue enjoys the cold, but that is because he once worked in Alaska as an ice-packer dog in a refrigeration factory. Or so he says. Actually, I am beginning to tire of his stories. This evening when I said that I wished that we had a telephone so that we could call up the rescue services to come and get us, Old Blue said that he could call them without a phone. Something to do with a special sense that all dogs have. He went on to explain that when dogs spray against a tree or a lamppost, they are really sending messages to all the other dogs who will later come along and sniff there. Old Blue said that he would send a message asking that we be rescued immediately. Really, what nonsense!

I am going to bed. Roo and Old Blue have just gone outside to send their messages up against a tree.

We are stuck here in a blizzard, Child, whether we like it or not.

Fear we may be stuck here for a long time yet . . .

Dear Child,

An extraordinary thing has happened. Woke up to the sounds of much barking. Staggered out of bed and went to take a look. The shack was surrounded by rescue dogs. There were dogs from the fire service, dogs from the coastguard, police dogs, huskies, a St Bernard and even two ambulance dogs with a stretcher. We have been rescued!

A police dog took all our details and said that a helicopter was on its way to fly us to Los Angeles. Said that the rescue message was picked up last night and passed through the dog bush telegraph straight to headquarters.

We packed up what was left of our luggage and went back out to wait for the helicopter.

Ted has promised to look after the duck for us and

the duck seemed more than happy to stay. It quacked as if to say so.

I thanked Ted for his hospitality and he gave me a piece of beef jerky to remember him by. I shall use it as a bookmark.

A tearful goodbye followed. Old Blue explained to Roo that he was never far away from her, no matter where she was. All she had to do was bark and he would come and find her. This made her feel a lot better. Then they chased each other in a big circle for the last time. I think that must be a dog's way of saying goodbye.

At last all our farewells were made and the helicopter landed beside Ted's shack. Old Blue and Ted watched as we climbed on board. Old Blue remarked that it was similar to a helicopter he had flown in Texas. Fortunately the pilot was a sensible chap and would not allow Old Blue to have 'a little spin'. We said goodbye for the last time, and Old Blue told Roo that he would write to her. Dogs can't write, I think everybody knows that, but it was a nice thing to say.

The pilot told Ted and Old Blue to stand back and then he started the engines.

As we pulled high above the trees in the helicopter, I could see Old Blue barking and running around in the snow. Then he stopped and looked up at us. He seemed to have written something in the snow with his tracks. It took a moment for me to work out what it actually said.

And so do I!